This Topsy and Tim book belongs to

_____

Topsy and Tim
Go to Hospital

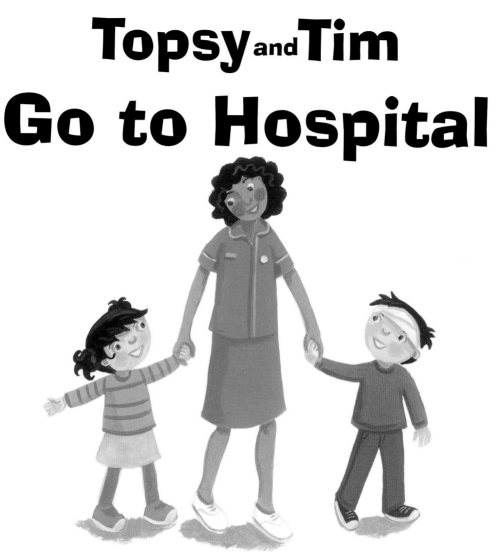

By Jean and Gareth Adamson

LADYBIRD BOOKS

UK | USA | Canada | Ireland | Australia
India | New Zealand | South Africa

Ladybird Books is part of the Penguin Random House group of companies
whose addresses can be found at global.penguinrandomhouse.com.
www.penguin.co.uk   www.puffin.co.uk   www.ladybird.co.uk

Penguin
Random House
UK

This title was previously published as part of the Topsy and Tim Learnabout series
Published by Ladybird Books Ltd
This edition 1999
Reissued 2010
009

Printed in China

A CIP catalogue record for this book is available from the British Library

ISBN: 978-1-409-30423-4

All correspondence to:
Ladybird Books
Penguin Random House Children's
One Embassy Gardens, New Union Square
5 Nine Elms Lane, London SW8 5DA

Tim was going to hospital. He had fallen out of a tree and bumped his head. Topsy and Mummy helped Tim to pack the things he would need in hospital.

The hospital was very big, with bedrooms called wards.
One ward had funny pictures on the walls.
"This must be the children's ward," said Mummy.
A nurse called Sister helped Tim put his things away in
his own special locker.

"The porter will take you to be photographed
in a minute," said Sister. "It will be an X-ray
photograph – the kind that shows what you
look like inside."

The porter came, pushing a big wheelchair
for Tim to sit in.
"Can Mummy come too?" asked Tim.
"Of course she can," said Sister.

It was a long way to the X-ray room.
Tim enjoyed his wheelchair ride.

He saw another porter pushing a little girl along.
She waved to Tim as they passed.

The lady who worked the X-ray camera stood behind a screen. She could see Tim through a little window.

Mummy stayed with Tim but she had
to wear a special apron. The X-ray
photograph was soon taken.

After lunch, the children went to
bed. Mummy tucked Tim in.
"Now I must go home to look after
Topsy," she said. "But don't worry,
I'll soon be back."

"Bring Topsy with you," said Tim.
"I will," said Mummy, but Tim didn't hear.
He was already fast asleep.

Topsy brought her best jigsaw puzzle when she came to see Tim in hospital. She thought he would like to play with it in bed.

Tim was not in bed. He was playing with the other children.

Tim took Topsy to meet his new friends.

On the way home, Topsy told Mummy she
had a pain – but she was not sure where it was.
Mummy did not believe her.
"I want to go to hospital too," said Topsy.

"Cheer up, Topsy," said Dad, when he came home from work. "I've brought a surprise present for you."

The surprise present was a medical set with
a syringe, a stethoscope and a thermometer.

When Topsy came home from school the
next day, she found Tim waiting for her.
"Mummy brought me home," said Tim.
"My head's all right now."

Soon every toy in the house was in Topsy and Tim's children's hospital.

*Now turn the page and help
Topsy and Tim solve a puzzle.*

Look at the toys below.
Can you find each of them
hidden in the big picture?

doll

teddy

car

marbles

book

ball

A Map of the Village

farm

Topsy and
Tim's house

Tony's
house

Kerr
hou

park

Have you read all the Topsy and Tim stories?

 Topsy and Tim — The New Baby
☐ 9781409300564

 Topsy and Tim — Have a Birthday Party
☐ 9781409300618

 Topsy and Tim — Go on an Aeroplane
☐ 9781409300571

 Topsy and Tim — Play Football
☐ 9781409303350

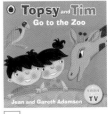 Topsy and Tim — Go on a Train
☐ 9781409304241

 Topsy and Tim — Learn to Swim
☐ 9781409300601

 Topsy and Tim — Start School
☐ 9781409300830

 Topsy and Tim — Go Camping
☐ 9781409303336

 Topsy and Tim — Go to Hospital
☑ 9781409304234

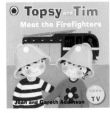 Topsy and Tim — Go to the Zoo
☐ 9781409300847

 Topsy and Tim — Go to the Dentist
☐ 9781409300588

 Topsy and Tim — At the Farm
☐ 9781409303367

 Topsy and Tim — Go to the Doctor
☐ 9781409303343

 Topsy and Tim — Have Itchy Heads
☐ 9781409307204

Topsy and Tim — Meet the Firefighters
☐ 9781409307211

Topsy and Tim — Safety First
☐ 9781409308829

Topsy and Tim — Meet the Police
☐ 9781409308836

 Topsy and Tim — Sports Day
☐ 9781409309468

Topsy and Tim — Visit London
☐ 9781409309475

Topsy and Tim — Meet Father Christmas
☐ 9781409311591

 Topsy and Tim — Help a Friend
☐ 9780723292593

 Topsy and Tim — Move House
☐ 9780723292586

 Topsy and Tim — First Sleepover
☐ 9780241189702

 Topsy and Tim — Have Their Eyes Tested
☐ 9780241282540

 Topsy and Tim — Go on Holiday
☐ 9780241282557

Jean and Gareth Adamson